My Little Book of
Emergency Vehicles

by Claudia Martin

QED

Quarto is the authority on a wide range of topics.
Quarto educates, entertains and enriches the lives of our readers—enthusiasts and lovers of hands-on living.
www.quartoknows.com

Publisher: Maxime Boucknooghe
Editorial Director: Victoria Garrard
Art Director: Miranda Snow
Editor: Sophie Hallam
Designer: Melissa Alaverdy

First published in the UK in 2016
by QED Publishing
Part of the The Quarto Group
The Old Brewery
6 Blundell Street
London N7 9BH

A catalogue record for this book is available from the British Library.

ISBN 978 1 78493 428 6

Printed in China

MIX
Paper from responsible sources
FSC® C101537
www.fsc.org

Words in **bold** are explained in the glossary on page 60.

Contents

Fire engines

When there's a fire, it is a fire engine's job to transport firefighters to the scene as quickly as possible.

>> **Most fire engines are red or another eye-catching colour.**

Everyone needs to get out of the way of a speeding fire engine! To catch your attention, fire engines have wailing sirens and flashing lights.

>> Fire engines carry equipment such as water, hoses and ladders.

⌄ 'Fire' is written backwards on this fire engine, so it can be read correctly in another driver's rear-view mirror.

Ladder trucks

A ladder truck has a ladder attached to its **chassis**. The ladder is extendable, which means it can slide open to get longer.

Ladder trucks are used to fight fires in tall buildings or to spray water onto blazes from above. Ladders may have a platform at the top where firefighters can stand.

⌃ **The longest ladders soar 112 metres into the air.**

≪ **This Bronto Skylift truck uses stabilizers to keep it from tipping over when its ladder is extended.**

Ladders are often on a turntable, so they can swivel.

FIRE RESCUE

30 M

28 FIRE

Airport crash tenders

Crash tenders are stationed at airports. They race into action if an aeroplane catches fire.

>> Tenders have all-wheel drive, **which means power is supplied to all wheels at once. This gives extra grip.**

⌄ The Rosenbauer Panther truck speeds up from 0 to 80 kilometres an hour in 25 seconds.

Aeroplanes carry lots of **flammable** fuel, so a fire can get out of control quickly. Crash tenders are equipped with large water tanks, **firefighting foam** and powerful sprays.

> ⌃ Crash tenders can spray water and foam a distance of 95 metres or more.

Wildland fire engines

A wildfire is a fire that rages in the countryside – in forest or grassland. Wildfires need a special type of fire engine.

>> A firefighter puts out a wildfire in the dry shrubland of southern France.

>> With its all-wheel drive, a wildland fire engine can speed across rough ground ahead of a fire.

Wildland fire engines have large water tanks and long hoses. Most fire engines have to stop before they pump water, but a wildland fire engine's pump works even as it races along.

∧ **The water tank of a standard wildland fire engine holds 1900 litres.**

Heavy rescue vehicles

These emergency **vehicles** carry rescue teams and their tools to car crashes or collapsed buildings.

⌄ **A rescue worker readies his tools at the site of an accident.**

⌃ **This Detroit Fire Department vehicle has a powerful Spartan cab and an SVI truck with plenty of storage.**

If someone is trapped in a car or another small space, the heavy rescue team will free them. They use tools such as cutters, spreaders and cranes.

↗ When it is fully loaded with equipment, a heavy rescue vehicle can weigh more than 20 tonnes.

Support vehicles

At the scene of a fire, you might spot other emergency vehicles, such as command units and tanker trucks.

⌄ **This firefighter is pumping water from a tanker to a fire engine. The fire engine will spray the water to put out the fire!**

A command unit is a specially fitted-out truck from which a fire chief can manage a crew. Inside the truck is communication equipment such as radios, telephones and computers.

⌃ This command unit is equipped with internet, radio and satellite links.

« A tanker truck's job is to hold extra water. It can fill up from a lake or a fire hydrant.

Firetrains

If a train catches fire, the quickest way to rescue passengers may be to use a special firefighting train.

⩔ **This firetrain is always ready for action in the Lötschberg railroad tunnel, which runs 34 kilometres beneath the Swiss Alps.**

<< A firetrain carries its own supply of air for breathing in smoky tunnels.

A firefighting train needs a powerful engine to pull a water tank and equipment wagon. The train can be split in two, with a second engine and ambulance wagon to carry passengers to a safe place.

⌃ The water tank of a Windhoff firetrain can hold 50,000 litres of water and foam.

Firefighting aircraft

Aeroplanes and helicopters are often used to drop water, firefighting foam, or **fire retardant** onto wildfires.

⌃ **A Lockheed P3 Orion aeroplane is spraying fire retardant onto a forest fire.**

« **This Bell "Huey" helicopter is scooping water from a lake, before carrying it to a fire.**

Some firefighting helicopters, called helitankers, have water tanks. Others carry a bucket for scooping water. Firefighting planes have tanks that are filled by a hose or by scooping water from a lake or river.

>> The tank of this Sikorsky S-70 "Firehawk" can hold 3700 litres of water.

Fireboats

Fireboats put out fires at sea, on board ships or on **oil rigs**. Sometimes they also battle blazes in harbours and on docks.

>> A New York City Fire Department boat shows off its water sprays.

Powerful water pumps and nozzles are the most important equipment for a fireboat. Some can spray water more than 120 metres into the air.

>> **Seven fireboats shoot water at a burning oil tanker, the *Mega Borg*.**

>> **At 43 metres long, *Fire Fighter II* is the United States' largest fireboat. It can pump nearly 200,000 litres of water per minute.**

21

Police cars

Police cars race through the streets to stop crimes and catch **suspects**. Cars usually have special markings, warning lights and a siren.

>> **A New York Police Department car speeds by with its lights flashing and its siren shrieking.**

<< **In the United Kingdom, police cars are often marked with checks in** high-visibility **yellow and blue.**

POLICE

<< Inside his patrol car, this officer is checking his computer to see if there are any emergencies.

The type of police car you are most likely to spot is a **patrol** car. These cars are used to patrol the streets and to respond to emergency calls.

Special police cars

When a police officer has a special task to do, they will need a special police car to do it!

>> **All-wheel drive SUVs can patrol beaches, parks or icy mountain roads.**

CA EXEMPT
1215146

警POLICE察

« **In Beijing, China, small electric cars are easier to drive on narrow streets and create less** pollution.

>> **Police dogs travel in this** station wagon, **in a caged area at the rear.**

Special police cars include **sports utility vehicles** (SUVs) for off-road driving, high-speed pursuit cars, electric cars for city patrols and unmarked cars for watching suspects.

Police vans

Police vans and trucks are used to transport police officers, prisoners and equipment – and to keep them safe inside.

>> This van has a wire shield that flips down to protect the windshield from objects being thrown.

<< In Washington DC, a bomb disposal team is on the move with their equipment.

When lots of officers need to reach the scene of a crime or a **riot**, they travel in a van. If they are facing a dangerous situation, the van may be armoured.

⌃ Covered in metal plates, these armoured police vans are ready for anything.

Police bikes

Motorcycles and bicycles can weave in and out of traffic – to get to the scene of an accident or crime quickly!

<< An Arizona Highway Patrol officer is standing by his Honda ST1300 motorcycle, which can travel 400 kilometres between fuel fill-ups.

<< This English police officer is riding a BMW R1200RT, which has a top speed of over 200 kilometres an hour.

Police motorcycles need to be fast but easy to control. Around the world, most police forces use BMW Motorrad, Harley-Davidson, Honda, Kawasaki and Yamaha motorcycles.

>> Although bicycles are slower than motorcycles, they are safer in crowded cities and create less pollution.

Police helicopters

Police helicopters are useful for giving a bird's-eye view of what is happening on the ground.

« Miami police officers take off in a Bell 206, which can fly at over 220 kilometres an hour.

Helicopters can watch traffic, track suspects and patrol large events. Officers in a helicopter are armed with **thermal imaging cameras**, which allow them to see in the dark.

>> **This two-engined Eurocopter Dauphin 2 is flown by the police force of Shizuoka, Japan.**

<< **A Eurocopter "Squirrel" helicopter patrols the skies above Sydney, Australia.**

Police boats

Harbours, lakes and rivers may be patrolled by police boats – from little inflatables to powerful speedboats.

⋎ Clyde Marine Police travel in an Arctic rigid inflatable boat (RIB). **RIBs have an air-filled collar, making them hard to sink.**

CHICA

Motor launches are often used for daily patrols. These are medium-sized boats that are powered by an engine. Sometimes super-fast speedboats are used to chase down fleeing suspects.

>> The sleek shape of this Spanish police speedboat lets it cut through the waves.

<< A motor launch is at work in a Chicago harbour.

Ambulances

Ambulances hurry to reach people who are sick or injured. It could be a matter of life and death!

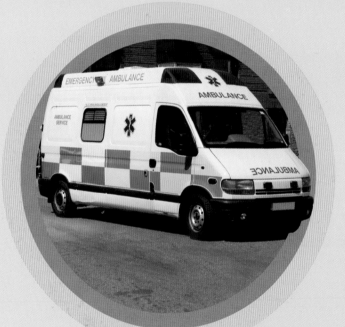

>> This ambulance is in a rush. The driver has turned on the flashing lights and siren.

⌃ In many countries, ambulances are brightly coloured and have special markings to make them hard to miss.

Ambulances are vans or trucks with plenty of room at the back for carrying patients, medical equipment and **paramedics**. Paramedics are trained to carry out life-saving treatment.

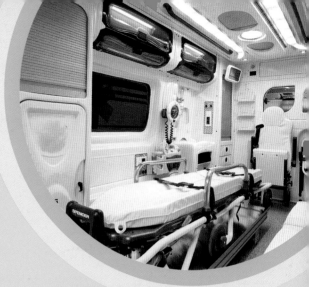

⌃ **Equipment includes stretchers, stethoscopes, medicine, bandages, oxygen for breathing and machines to help heart problems.**

Ambulance buses

If there is an earthquake or flood, many people could need medical help. This situation calls for an ambulance bus.

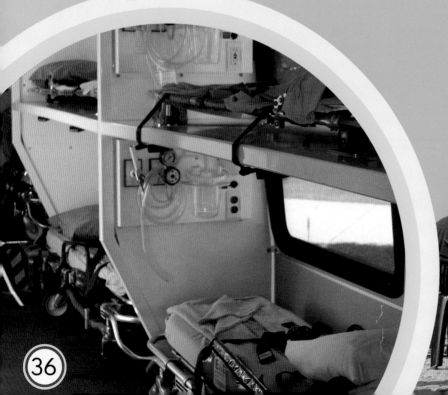

« The largest ambulance buses have 24 beds.

From the outside, an ambulance bus may look like any other bus. Inside, it is fitted out as a mini-hospital so that injured people can be cared for on the spot.

« You might see an ambulance bus parked at a large event, just in case anyone needs treatment.

Paramedic bikes

When traffic is heavy, a paramedic on a motorcycle or bicycle can reach an emergency much more quickly than one in a car or van.

<< **The Piaggio MP3 three-wheeled scooter is used by Israeli paramedics.**

>> **This motorcycle ambulance has its warning lights on as it zips between buses and cars in London, England.**

Paramedic motorcycles and bicycles have large side boxes or bags, called panniers. Panniers hold medical supplies and a defibrillator. A defibrillator is a machine that can restart the heart.

⌃ In crowded cities, it can be safer to send paramedics on bicycles than motorcycles. These paramedics work in Los Angeles.

Air ambulances

There's an emergency in a traffic-clogged city. Or maybe someone is hurt on a distant island. It's time for the air ambulance.

>> **The Royal Flying Doctors of Australia use this Beechcroft Super King aeroplane for long-distance emergencies.**

<< **An air ambulance has landed in a central London park.**

Helicopters can land in places that cannot be easily reached by road – such as mountaintops and busy city centres. Aeroplanes can travel long distances quickly, so they are often used to reach remote spots.

G-OEMT

EAST ANGLIAN AIR AMBULANCE

SURGICAL AIRWAY

⌃ **This MBB/Kawasaki BK117 helicopter ambulance travels at over 250 kilometres an hour.**

Water ambulances

If you live on a little island or by the sea, the quickest way to reach a hospital could be by boat.

>> **The USNS *Mercy* hospital ship has 12** operating rooms **and beds for 1000 patients.**

Water ambulances are usually small, fast motorboats. But if there is a major disaster or war, a giant hospital ship may arrive at the coast to treat injured people.

≪ *Flying Christine III* works as an ambulance around the island of Guernsey in the English Channel. It is 14 metres long.

⋁ Water ambulances speed along the canals of Venice, Italy, which is built on 118 small islands.

AMBULANZA

6V30155

1.1.8

FURUNO

All-weather lifeboats

All-weather lifeboats and their crews brave towering waves and howling winds to reach ships and boats that are in trouble at sea.

>> **This all-weather lifeboat works for the United States** Coast Guard.

⌄ **In stormy seas off the English coast, this** RNLI **Severn-class lifeboat can take 128 passengers.**

Even in a storm, all-weather lifeboats are large enough and strong enough to travel far out to sea. They are built so that, if they overturn, they can quickly roll upright again.

Inshore lifeboats

Smaller 'inshore' lifeboats rescue people who need help close to the shore. They can work near dangerous rocks and cliffs.

⌄ **This RNLI rigid inflatable boat is at work off the coast of England.**

Rigid inflatable boats are often used as inshore lifeboats. Their air-filled collar makes them very stable, even in breaking waves. Other inshore lifeboats include small motor launches and hovercrafts.

⌃ **This US Coast Guard inshore lifeboat has a strong aluminium hull. It is 7.6 metres long.**

⌃ **Hovercraft travel over land or water on a cushion of air. They are used for rescues on mudflats or in very shallow water.**

Patrol boats

Patrol boats criss-cross the world's oceans, looking out for pirates, **smugglers** and ships that need help.

<< A US Coast Guard Marine Protector boat carries weapons and a rigid inflatable boat.

>> At 150 metres long, the Japan Coast Guard's *Shikishima* is one of the world's biggest patrol ships.

⌄ **This ship patrols Russian waters. It has liferafts, cranes and diving equipment.**

Most countries have a **navy**, coast guard or police force to send out patrol boats. The largest patrol boats carry lifeboats, helicopters, medical equipment – and even weapons!

RESCUER

RESCUE ZONE

Lifeguard vehicles

Lifeguards work at the beach, ready to rescue swimmers who need help. Sometimes lifeguards leap onto speedy emergency vehicles!

« These Australian lifeguards are using a motorboat to keep an eye on surfers.

A **quad bike** or all-wheel drive truck will get a lifeguard across the beach faster than running. A **jet ski** or small motorboat can race over the waves more quickly than a swimmer.

⌃ With four wheels, a quad bike is stable even on bumpy sand.

⌃ A lifeguard on a Yamaha Waverunner jet ski plucks a struggling swimmer from the water.

Air-sea rescue

Air-sea rescue teams use helicopters and aeroplanes to search for and rescue people who are in danger at sea.

⊻ **This HC13OP Hercules plane can drop liferafts and rescuers wearing parachutes. Here it is dangling a hose to refuel a rescue helicopter.**

Aircraft often work alongside rescue boats, using equipment such as thermal imaging cameras. Rescue swimmers may need to leap into the water to grab hold of survivors.

⌄ **A Canadian Cormorant helicopter is working side by side with a rescue boat.**

≫ **A US Coast Guard HH-60 Jayhawk helicopter dangles a brave rescue swimmer.**

Amphibious rescue

Amphibious vehicles can travel on both land and water. They are often used for rescuing people from floods.

⋁ **The Arktos rescue craft can travel on water, ice, rocky ground and quicksand.**

<< These Russian "Blue Bird" vehicles rescue spacecraft that touch down in water.

Amphibious vehicles are built to float and be stable in water. Some have air-filled cushions to help. On land, they travel on tracks or wheels.

⌃ A tracked amphibious vehicle is rescuing people from a flood. Tracks stop its wheels from sinking into soft ground.

Mountain rescue

If someone is lost or hurt in the mountains, it's the job of a mountain rescue team to save them.

>> A snowmobile is perfect for taking a paramedic to fallen skiers. It runs on tracks, with skis at the front for steering.

Mountain rescue teams have to deal with snow, steep cliffs and storms. They often use helicopters to land on mountaintops or to lift people to safety using ropes.

⌃ **This all-wheel drive Toyota Land Cruiser carries out search and rescue in Iceland.**

⌄ **This rescue dog travels by helicopter. It's his job to sniff out people who are buried by avalanches.**

Tugs and tow trucks

They may be unlikely heroes, but tugboats and tow trucks can save our environment – and even our lives.

⌄ **This tug is towing the leaking oil tanker *Exxon Valdez* away from the reef where it ran aground.**

« A Mercedes-Benz tow truck is rescuing a car from a flood.

Tugboats are strong little boats that can tow much larger ships. They drag damaged ships and oil tankers away from danger. They can even pump up spilled oil before it kills sea creatures.

» A tugboat leads a giant container ship through a narrow harbour.

Glossary

all-wheel drive When power is supplied to all a vehicle's wheels at once, giving extra grip on uneven surfaces. Other vehicles have front-wheel drive or rear-wheel drive.

bomb disposal How dangerous explosives are made safe.

cab The driver's compartment in a van or truck.

chassis The metal frame of a motor vehicle, which supports the engine, wheels and body.

coast guard An organization that saves lives and makes sure laws are obeyed at sea.

fire hydrant A water pipe, usually in the street, where firefighters can attach hoses.

fire retardant A liquid or gel that slows the spread of a fire.

firefighting foam A foam that is sprayed onto a fire to put it out.

flammable Easily set on fire.

high-visibility A bright colour that appears to glow in the dark.

jet ski A small engine-driven water vehicle on which the driver sits or stands.

motor launch A boat driven by an engine, with a hull (body) that is open or partly covered by a deck.

navy The part of a country's armed forces that works at sea.

oil rig A platform in the sea with equipment for drilling into the seabed for oil.

operating room A room where doctors carry out operations.

paramedic A person who is trained to give emergency medical care.

patrol To keep watch over an area by travelling around it.

pollution Waste materials that harm the air, water or soil.

quad bike A motorcycle with four large wheels that can be driven on rough ground.

rigid inflatable boat (RIB) A boat with a solid hull (body) and an air-filled collar.

riot Wild or violent behaviour by a crowd of people.

RNLI Royal National Lifeboat Institution; an organization that sends out lifeboats around the coasts of the United Kingdom.

smuggler Someone who brings goods into a country illegally.

sports utility vehicle (SUV) A large automobile or van with all-wheel drive.

stabilizer A prop that keeps a vehicle steady.

station wagon An automobile with a large area behind the seats, reached by a door at the rear.

suspect A person who is thought to have committed a crime.

thermal imaging camera A camera that shows the heat given off by people and vehicles.

turntable A round platform that can be turned.

vehicle A machine used for travelling on land, in water or in the air.

Index

Picture credits

(t=top, b=bottom, l=left, r=right, c=center, fc=front cover, bc=back cover)

Alamy: 5br © HOT SHOTS, 10br, 10-11, 14bl © FORGET Patrick/SAGAPHOTO.COM, 12bl Oberhaeuser AgencyAgencja Fotograficzna Caro, 12-13 Marvin Debinsky Photo Associates, 13tr © IAN MARLOW / Alamy, 14-15 blue light images / Alamy, 15cr ABN Images, 34-35 B Christopher / Alamy, 38-39 © one-image photography / Alamy, 43tl © Robert Smith / Alamy, © Chris Slack / Alamy, 54bc Robert McLean, © ITAR-TASS Photo Agency

Corbis: 6cr Guy Spangenberg/Transtock, 6-7 Darren Greenwood/Design Pics, 20-21 © Ralf-Finn Hestoft, 21tr, 58 © Bettmann/CORBIS, 21bc ©Robert Sciarrino/The Star-Ledger/Star Ledger, 22bl © Mark Kerrison/Demotix, 23tc ©DiMaggio/Kalish, 23 ©Amanda Hall/Robert Harding World Imagery, 28-29, 40-41 © Martyn Goddard, 30bl © Carl & Ann Purcell/CORBIS, 30-31 © HO/Reuters, 36bl © Zoran Milich/Masterfile, 40-41 David Spurdens, 42-43 © Carlo Morucchio/Robert Harding World Imagery, 44bc ANDREW MILLS/Star Ledger, 44-45

Dreamsitme: 6bl ID26016063 © Bobbrooky, 8-9, 29tl © Martin Brayley, 24bc ©Wangkun Jia, 24-25 © Wpd911, 25tr © Kevin Chesson, 26bl © Kiraly Istvan Daniel, 26-27 © Rkaphotography, 29br © Julie Feinstein, 33cr © Typhoonski, 34cl © Timothy Large, 38 bl © Vebaska, 57tc © Einarmeme, 59tl © Taina Sohlman, 59bc © Alptraum

Getty: 4-5 photosbyjim, 5tr Great Art Productions Photographer's Choice, 18bl GavinD, 18-19 Shari L. Morris, 27cr epixx, 32-33 Hisham Ibrahim Photographer's Choice RF, 36-37 Tramino, 42cr Stocktrek Images, 46-47 Neil Holmes Photolibrary, 50-51 Joss Joss Collection:Perspectives, 51tr JULIE THURSTON PHOTOGRAPHY, 52bc, 52-53 Pete Ryan, 53cr U.S. COAST GUARD, 54-55 STR, 56-57 FangXiaNuo, 57bc Tom Bear

Shutterstock: 1c ID1974, 2-3c aragami12345s, 46bl silvergull, 47tr Gary Paul Lewis, 48br KAI AYASE, 48-49 ID1974, 50 bl ChameleonsEye, 60-61 Eugene Berman, 63br PlusONE, 64br AnnaIA

Wikimedia Commons: 8bl Altenburg-Nobitz_Airport_Rosenbauer_Panther, 9tr Water_cannon_salute_Ryanair_RJK_15042011, 11tr Brush_28_of_PBCFR, 16bl Rettungszug, 16-17 Windhoff_Fire_Fighting_and_Rescue_Train, 17tl FFS_XT-mas_99_85_9174_004-3_StSaphorin, 19cr Lacos70-N160LA-040501-01, 31tr Shizuoka_Police_JA22PC_Eurocopter_AS365N1_Dauphin-2_RJNY, 32bl Police_of_the_Clyde_Marine_Unit_on_Escort_Duties_Near_Faslane,_Scotland_MOD_45152120, 35tr Ambulanza_Italiana_2010_vano_sanitario, 39cr Bicycle_Paramedics, 40cr VH-FDA_Beechcraft_B200_Super_King_Air_Royal_Flying_Doctor_Service_of_Australia, 48cr USCGC_Cormorant